Murder By Moonlight

It was a Friday night in the small rural town of Palm Grove, with six hundred people. Mangrove trees are surrounded by thick Bushland on the banks of the Brackish River.

The Full Moon was bright, casting a long silver streak across the water to the Driftwood Hotel, which, as it happens, is an old Mangrove tree with an 8m X 2m table where the locals meet after work to enjoy a beer and a yarn.

Five minutes drive out of town heading to Dullich, the next major city, there is an abandoned animal rescue station called Evergreen Hills, a sanctuary that housed injured animals; pens, cages, and yards once used to rehabilitate and release them back into the wild.

At Evergreen Hills, there's an old fibro building with an office in the front and an operating room in the back; Arayah had worked there as a wildlife coordinator before the local council closed it for much-needed refurbishment.

There were no clouds this particular night. The river was calm and still, almost glass-looking,

Arayah is 5ft 8in, with Hazel eyes, long golden blonde hair, and a perfect likeness to her late mother. Arayah was already at the hotel when Her boyfriend Garrett, a 6-foot man with a ginger beard that was slowly graying and ginger hair, was madly in love with Arayah, although she couldn't see why; she was nothing special. Nevertheless, Garrett loved her; he could see her inner beauty.

Garrett sat next to Arayah and kissed her hello, then cracked his first beer; turning to Arayah, he asked, "Did you hear a scream last night? It was a blood-curdling scream that sounded like it came from a woman.

"Nah, I didn't hear a thing; as soon as my head hit the pillow, I was out to it,"

Arayah replied

Garrett asked, "How could you not have heard it? It sounded like it came right behind where you live."

That was true enough; Arayah lived right behind Evergreen Hills.

"You don't suppose someone is squatting there? I mean, it wouldn't be the first time."

Inquired Arayah

"I guess it's possible," Garrett replied

"Wanna come and check it out."

"Oh, I dunno; what if we see something we shouldn't."

"I'll protect you; let's go."

Arayah reluctantly followed Garrett to his Jet Black F350 truck.

They drove to Evergreen hills, and arriving at the main gate, they both noticed smoke coming from the back of the building near the rehabilitation pens.

"Well, that can't be good," stated Garrett

"I hope nothing alive was in there," Arayah said in a state of panic

Arayah had seen dead people before; after all, she found her mum when she died, and she had tried in vain to resuscitate her beloved fiancee, who passed away beside her in bed one night; so, seeing the dead was nothing new to her; however, seeing a burning body was something entirely different. Arayah didn't know how she would handle that

"let's go see; it may be nothing to worry about," Garrett said

"Yeah, but it could be that woman you heard," Arayah said, concerned

"Stop worrying; I'm here." Garret's voice was shaky. Arayah could tell he was just as scared as she was. He tried not to show it, though that wasn't much comfort for Arayah, who had a lump in her throat and a knot in her stomach.

Neither one knew what they were about to find; they just knew that curiosity got them; they had to go and investigate.

Garrett and Arayah reached the back of the main building; by now, the flames were higher than they first saw from the main entrance. Through the thick smoke haze, Garrett saw burning pallets and rags; he called to Arayah,

"it's OK; there are just rags and pallets burning."

Arayah walked over to garret and put her face in his chest; Arayah could not bring herself to look at the flames; Garrett, on the other hand, seemed fixated by the flames flickering in front of him.

"It's OK, babe. It's just general rubbish burning away."

"Phew,"

Arayah said, looking at the fire. "We should put it out though"

Garrett said as he walked away to look for a bucket or hose.

Garrett noticed a skip bin beside the stockyards; he looked inside, thinking there might be something to extinguish the fire.

Throwing trash and building materials this way, he found an old plastering bucket. As he pulled the handle, something fell out with a loud thump as it hit the bottom of the skip bin.

It was loud enough that Arayah heard it from a short distance away,

"What was that?" she called

"I dunno, probably a brick or something,"

he replied as he reached into his pocket to get his mobile phone to use as a torch.

As soon as he shone the torch, he saw what was in the bucket. He called out to Arayah,

"Stay where you are, do not come over."

In a scared voice, Arayah asked "What is it? What's wrong?"

Arayah headed over to Garrett. He had stopped her just as she was about to look inside

"You don't want to see this, honey," he said in a reassuring voice.

Turning towards the truck, they noticed a shadow in the doorway.

The shadow was holding a lit cigarette in its mouth. You could see the end glow as the shadow inhaled,

The shadow stepped out of the doorway into the moonlight,

"Jesus, Maverick, you scared the daylights out of us. What in the hell are you doing here?"

Maverick was eighty-two, homeless, and had a well-known identity around Palm Grove.

"I was fishing, then I started to get cold, so I came over here to get warm, and well, I guess I fell asleep."

"How long have you been here?"

Asked Arayah

"I dunno, maybe 5 hours, give or take," Maverick replied, looking at his watch.

"Did you hear or see anything?"

Questioned Garrett.

"Nah, Mate, not a damn thing."

Maverick glanced in Arayah's Direction with a smirk

Garrett escorted Arayah back to his truck and told her to wait until he returned.

Garrett then returned to Maverick.

By now, the moon's light was bright enough for them to see inside the skip bin.

Maverick and Garrett peered inside to discover to their dismay, a Severed head that once belonged to a female

Blood soaked her thick curly blonde hair. There were deep gashes in her beautiful olive complexioned skin, so deep that you could see her cheekbones.

The eyes, they say, are the windows to the soul; these eyes, these deep brown eyes, looked like they knew pain and sorrow.

She had no makeup on, not that she needed it.

"Whaddaya suppose happened to her, Garrett.?"

Maverick inquired

God only knows, Mate." Garrett replied, "whoever did this was mighty angry about

something; you don't do this kind of damage lightly."

Garrett pulled his phone out to call the police, "oh damn it to hell."

"what's the matter.?" Maverick asked

"My phone's dead; the torch was left on and drained the bloody battery," Garrett said

Just as they were about to head to the truck, Maverick noticed something glistening in the bin; he reached in, moved a pile of newspapers, and found a severed arm; the thing glistening in the moonlight was a diamond ring on her left middle finger.

Maverick turned around and vomited on his sneakers.

"This is a seriously messed up situation here," Maverick said as he wiped his mouth with the sleeve of his jacket.

"You got that right; I need to call the Cops," Garrett replied

Garrett and Maverick returned to the F350 to find that Arayah was not there. "For crying out loud, where the hell is she? I don't have time for this."

Just as Garrett opened the door to his truck: he heard a terrifying scream. He started running towards the sound; just as Arayah was about to

faint, he caught her, gently guiding her to the ground; he said to Maverick, "Gimme your Jacket."

Maverick removed his jacket and gave it to Garrett, "well, this is great. Why couldn't she stay where I told her to?"

Maverick asked Garrett for the keys.

"I'll get help, and you stay here with Arayah."

With that, Maverick left. (What felt like forever, but was maybe 2 hours), Maverick returned with an entourage of emergency services. There was also a crowd of locals gathering.

The police arrived a brief time later to control the ever-growing crowd, hoping to catch a glimpse of what was happening.

Travis Le Roux was 53, 5 ft 4, has a stocky build, black cropped hair, beard, and mustache; Le Roux has been a 30-year veteran and the senior homicide Detective at Dullich police station; he was the first on the scene to look at the remains before questioning Garrett, who was sitting with his legs stretched out, with Arayah's head on his lap. He stroked her hair, telling her, it's OK, I'm here, you're OK.

Le Roux asked the paramedic to give Arayah something to bring her around. She had been

out to it for an hour. Le Roux had questions that needed answers.

Almost at once after the Adrenalin, Arayah woke up; she was groggy and a little hazy

"What's happened? What's going on? Where am I?'

"You are at the abandoned animal sanctuary. Unfortunately, there has been an accident." Garrett said in a calm, soothing voice.

In a state of confusion, Arayah asked, "who are all these people?"

"Forensics, we are here to examine and secure the crime scene. There has been a Gruesome Murder." Replied Le Roux

With tears in her eyes, Arayah asks, "Who is it, who is dead.?"

"I Don't know; I haven't seen them around here before," Garrett said.

The local news crew was reporting from across the road.

"We are reporting live from Palm Grove. This small town is the site of a brutal and gruesome murder. Our sources tell us that the victim is an unknown female, approximately 42 years of age, with curly blonde hair, brown eyes, and an olive complexion. We will stay on scene and report to you live as more information

becomes known. I'm Kerrigan Yates for Channel 9 NEWS."

Dawn was breaking, shedding an orange glow on the skip bin that held the remains of the mystery woman when Arayah asked if she could go to the toilet and freshen up.

Detective Le Roux snapped his fingers and pointed in the direction of Officer Riley.

"Can you escort -I'm sorry, Miss; what's your name again?"

"I'm A-A-Arayah," she stuttered, "Yes, Arayah, can you escort her to the lavatory, please?"

This way, thanks, Officer Riley motioned

"I know where it is; I used to work here before they closed it for maintenance," Arayah remarked.

"Officer Riley, May I ask you a question?" "What is it.?"

"Have you ever seen anything so gruesome in your time on the force.?"

"I've been on the force fifteen years, I've seen a lot, but nothing quite this disturbing- this is almost something out of a horror movie. I nearly launched my lunch at the sight of that poor woman. I can't say I've ever seen a dismembered body."

"Do You think she knew her killers? Will you catch them, do you reckon.?"

"I can't say whether she knew her killer/s; however, I can tell you, most definitely, we will catch whoever did this, mark my words."

Arayah looked like she was a little terrified but quickly brushed it off before closing the bathroom door behind her.

Moments later, Riley knocked on the door. Arayah? are you in there?

No reply Arayah?

Still no reply. Riley stepped back and raised her leg, ready to kick the door down with a BANG! The door flew open. Riley found Arayah sitting with her head in her hands, quietly sobbing; Riley heard Arayah mumble something, but she couldn't hear what it was.

Detective Le Roux was interviewing Garrett. When Riley and Arayah returned, Garrett looked in the direction of Arayah and smiled. Riley wondered what that smile meant and took a mental note; she would report what she saw the Le Roux later. She looked after Arayah, who had no idea she was actually a suspect herself, as were Garrett and Maverick.

"Hey Le Roux, come over here," Dennis, one of the crews, called, to which Le Roux said to Garrett, "You stay here; I'll be right back," as he walked over to the skip bin.

"Look at this." handing Le Roux an evidence bag with a scrunched-up photograph smeared with blood.

"What do you make of this?"

"It looks like our Victim, but I can't make out who the other person is – give it to the lab and tell them to put a rush on it."

"Will do." Replied Dennis

Le Roux returned to find Arayah and Garrett whispering to each other

"Oi, what do You two think you are doing? "We're just chatting." They replied in unison. "More like getting your stories straight." "Are we a suspect?" Asked Garrett

"Yes, you are, Now, you go over there," looking at Arayah, and you stay where you are

Riley, Keep an eye on those two, will you? And if they move, Arrest them both.

Le Roux turned around to see the coroner pull up to take the body back to Redmead.

Le Roux walked up to Roscoe and shook his hand,

"G'day Ross, it's been a while. How are the grand-kids?

"Yeah, not too bad, so what have you got for me?"

"A bloody and gruesome Murder – One of the worst I've seen in a long time." Le Roux said, shaking his head."

We found a head and an arm so far belonging to an unknown female; the cause of death is likely to be decapitation."

Roscoe scoffs, "That's for me to decide, don't you think?"

"Yeah, I 'spose, just trying to help." I don't need your help, Le Roux." Roscoe calls Dennis,

"Has anyone searched for the rest of this poor woman's body?

"Nup, we were told to wait for you."

"Well, get a hazmat suit on and start searching."

"Roger that." Said Dennis.

Roscoe went to the van and returned with evidence bags and a body bag to put the victim's remains in to transport her body securely.

He gently placed her head and arm in the bag while his assistant Bryce photographed everything he felt was pertinent to the case.

Roscoe also put various pieces of newspaper and debris into evidence bags.

He turned to speak to his assistant when he noticed someone who was not on his team.

"WHO THE HELL ARE YOU." He yelled

"Kerrigan Yates, Channel 9 NEWS, care to comment?"

"SOMEONE, GET THIS IDIOT OUT OF HERE BEFORE SHE CONTAMINATES THE CRIME SCENE."

Riley ran to Kerrigan and ushered her away "You can't be here; this is a crime scene."

It's OK. I've got what I need,"" Kerrigan replied as she left.

While Riley was removing Kerrigan from the scene, Arayah had vanished.

Upon returning to Garrett, Riley inquired about the whereabouts of Arayah.

""How should I know? You were supposed to be watching her, weren't you?""

""Don't get smart with me."

Riley Approached Le Roux; she was dreading this conversation; she had never lost a witness until now in the 15 years she had been an officer. She knew this was a terrible thing to happen. This event was going on her previously unblemished record. Riley was sure of it.

Why didn't I wait for someone else to get rid of Kerrigan, she thought as she stopped in front of Le Roux.

"Excuse me, sir?" she began, "I've - um – well

- oh hell - I've," stammered Riley

"Spit it out, Riley," Le Roux said, growing impatient.

"I've lost the witness."

"YOU DID WHAT? - WHICH ONE?"

The Woman, Arayah."

"Jesus, Riley, how'd you manage that.?"

"Roscoe called for someone to remove a reporter, and without thinking, I ran over to do it."

"Son of a Bitch, at least ten other people could have done that. Your job was to keep an eye on the witnesses, nothing more."

Le Roux crouched down to tie his shoe. In doing so, he spoke quietly, "You can expect a reprimand from the commissioner for this foul-up. Do you hear me, Riley?"

"Yes, Sir."

"NOW GO FIND HER." He yelled With that, Riley went over to Garrett,

From the way Riley was questioning him, he felt it bordered on intimidation. But on the other hand, he knew Riley felt frustrated and humiliated, she had one job, and she somehow managed to screw it up.

Riley called in the dog squad to help track Arayah's whereabouts. It appeared, however, that she was no longer in proximity.

This is going to be more challenging than I thought, Riley muttered.

"Over here,"

one of the searchers called from a stockyard next to the skip bin.

Riley raced over, thinking it was Arayah, only to find that it was another piece of the victim had been located

"Oh, dear God," Riley cried.

The torso had been found. There were deep wounds to the victim's stomach and chest.

"Who would do something so cruel and callous?"

The perp was angry. And wanted this woman to suffer, thought Riley.

"I can almost guarantee there's more of her around here." Said Roscoe.

The skeletal remains of her legs were found in the fire.

There was an unused operating room near where the fire was.

This is where it happened, the brutal Murder.

As you walked in, you could see and smell the crime scene. Blood dripped off the sides of the large metal operating table to the right, forming a congealed puddle on the floor below.

To the left of the table was a blood-stained sink with recently used surgical instruments.

Raquel, a capable and experienced crime scene agent, noticed a large stainless steel bone saw covered with bits of flesh and blood, though it's unclear if it was an animal or a Human.

"let's get this to the lab for testing." So said Raquel, carefully placing the saw into an evidence bag.

Garrett was detained and driven to Redmead Police Station for further questioning, leaving Riley free to look for Arayah, who had disappeared without a trace.

After an extensive search of adjacent properties and Bush land, the local Fire Service water division tasked to help search creeks, inlets and boats also searched to no avail.

The search had almost finished when Riley decided to check a dilapidated boat at the end of the mooring field, the "River Rose," Garrett's Cabin Cruiser. In the engine bay, Arayah was found and later arrested for escaping police custody and trying to pervert the course of justice.

Back at the station in Redmead, Arayah was photographed and fingerprinted as a process of elimination. Specific charges were pending as they were dependent on the outcome of the murder investigation.

Riley and Arayah sat in the interview room for nine and a half hours when Arayah asked if she could have something to eat and drink.

Feeling tired and stressed, Riley agreed. During their meal, Arayah asked where Garrett was.

"No need to worry. Garrett is fine; let's get back to it, shall we.?"

"Tell me about Friday night." "Well," began Arayah

I was at the local hotel, where people spend time together on a Friday night, well, any day or night of the week; Garrett and a few others were there. Around 11pm, Garrett asked if I wanted to check out Evergreen Hills because He had heard a scream the previous night, I wasn't too keen, but Garrett said I would be OK

"How did Garrett come to hear a scream?"

Riley interjected

"I don't know, really: he asked me if I heard anything. I told him I hadn't," continued Arayah

We drove to the main gate and noticed the fire. We decided to drive up and check it out. The flames were higher than we first thought

We went to have a look and found that rags and pallets were burning,

Garrett and I searched for water to put the fire out with.

That's when Garrett found something in the bucket. Unfortunately, the victim's head fell out into the skip bin.

"After the head was discovered, what happened?" Riley asked

"We were about to leave to get help when we noticed a shadow in the doorway."

"Who was the shadow?" queried Riley

"Garrett said Maverick and asked him what he was doing there," Maverick said he was fishing and got cold, so he came over to get warm

Riley wrote Maverick's name down on her pad. Just as the interview room door opened, Riley stopped the interview recorder to speak to Detective Le Roux

"Interview stopped so Officer could speak to Detective Le Roux and walked over to the door.

Le Roux then entered the room and sat opposite Arayah; He started the tape-recording, stating, "Detective Le Roux enters the room to continue the interview with Arayah."

Le Roux spoke in a calm tone

"We've had a breakthrough in the case. It has become known that the photograph found in the victim's hand is, in fact, our victim. It had been confirmed who the second person was. It's you, isn't it?"

Arayah started crying. With tears rolling down her cheeks, she answered sadly

"Yes, it's me. The woman is my Ex-Lover Mysti: we had been dating for five years off and on. Before I met Garret, we broke up, and Mysti never got over it. She's been stalking us ever since."

"Did you kill her?" Le Roux asked directly

"Oh god no, I could never do that. I loved her, Arayah replied, still sobbing.

"If not you, then who?" Detective Le Roux quizzed,

"isn't that your job to find out?" asked Arayah

Officer Riley entered the room. "Sir, it is getting late."

"Yes, and your point?"

"Nothing. I was just wondering how long we would be."

Why do you have somewhere else to be, Riley? Detective Le Roux asked agitatedly

"I Feel like I'm going to pass out," Arayah interjected

As soon as Arayah said that, she hit the cold hard floor of the interview room

"Riley, GET THE DOCTOR NOW"

Le Roux called

Riley left the room and returned a short time later with Doctor Vernon

"Riley tells me you have a patient for me."

"There she is, Le Roux," said, pointing to the floor.

"This is Arayah. She's a suspect in a homicide."

Detective Le Roux explained

"Has she had any drugs or Medication?" Vernon inquired

Riley explained that Arayah had gone to the bathroom at Evergreen hills, "the door was closed. I can neither confirm nor deny whether she did," but that was twelve hours ago.

Wouldn't it have been more immediate if she took something then?"

"Her breathing is shallow, and her pulse is weak. We need to call an ambulance." Vernon continued

While waiting for the ambulance to arrive, Dr. Vernon gave Arayah ten Micro grams of Narcan, a drug given to people suspected of overdose, just in case Arayah had taken something that made her pass out.

Within minutes, Arayah came to. In a state of confusion, she asked

"what's going on? Where am I?"

Dr. Vernon replied

"You were found in the engine bay on River Rose, do you remember?"

"I remember being at Evergreen Hills earlier and just now when I woke up on the floor of this room."

"What's happening, she sobbed"

Sympathetically Le Roux replied, "I don't know, but we will get to the bottom of this. We are waiting on an ambulance to take you to the hospital."

"Why there's nothing wrong with me. It's been a long and emotionally draining day. I'm just tired, that's all."

"I beg to differ. This is the second time you have passed out. Officer Riley will be your escort to and from the hospital and phone me with the results.

"Oh, and Riley, keep an eye on her this time. Can you do that?"

"Yes, sir"

Arayah and Riley arrived at the hospital, blood was taken, and the results were given to Riley within a few hours, who proceeded to telephone Detective Le Roux.

"Riley here, sir."

"Yes, I have the results."

"No, besides being dehydrated and slightly anemic, there is nothing illicit in her system."

"Yes, sir, understood."

"We will see you back at the station."
"Good-bye"

Riley returned to Arayah and escorted her back to the station. On the way, Riley had told her what Detective Le Roux had said

"You are free to go home, but you can't leave town."

Two days later, the police media liaison officer Super Intendant Richard Holloway had come to do a press conference.

Holloway hadn't been on the force for as long as Travis. He knew, however, about violent crime. And has been involved in operation

Jilliby, a secret task force that ran out of Dullich to apprehend gangs during the constant Gangland turf wars. So many nights, Richard would arrive home late or sometimes not at all, as He was up for long hours doing a stakeout or observing the goings on around the various locations that the gangs were frequenting.

By now, the Autopsy had been conducted, and the results of the lab tests were concluded.

Good morning, I'm Superintendent Holloway from the Special Crime Unit,

On Saturday morning, Detectives were called to Evergreen Hills to investigate a Heinous and Cruel Murder of an unknown female victim. I am not a liberty to say how or when she died, but I can say that this is one of the most vicious and calculated murders I have seen. We have several people helping us with our inquiries. We are obtaining a search warrant for a person of interest at this stage.

I have nothing further to add at this point in time.

Thank -you

Riley had returned from Dullich courthouse with the search warrant to search the premises of Garrett William Jarvis.

Riley handed the search warrant to Le Roux, who walked over to his team.

"Right, ready to move out? I'll take the lead. Riley, you head over to Arayah's and bring her back here."

Garrett was sitting on his front porch with a beer when the police arrived.

Le Roux stepped out of the car, walked to Garrett, and handed him the search warrant.

"This is bullshit. I aint done nuttin' wrong." "SIT DOWN, GARRETT" Le Roux yelled

The Search team walked out of Garrett's' house and shed with arms full of boxes, bags, and alike.

A look of panic came over Garrett's' face when he saw an officer walk out with a square metal box, about the size of a small suitcase

"Oi, you can't take that. It doesn't even open. I lost the keys to it years ago when my mum gave it to me."

Garrett went to stand up and walk down the stairs, but Le Roux looked sternly at him, so he sat back down.

Jesus, I may need a lawyer, Garrett thought As he pulled his mobile out of his pocket.

"I'll take that Le Roux said, holding his arm and hand open.

"I was just going to call my lawyer," Garrett explained

"You can do that at the station."

Back at the station, Superintendent Holloway was conducting a press release.

"The remains of a 42-year-old woman had been found. I can confirm that the victim was Mysti Renee Dawkins of Little halt was found at Evergreen Hills animal rescue station Last Friday morning. I cannot confirm how she died. I can, however, say that it was gruesome,

and she had suffered quite a bit. I'll open
to questions now."

"Kerrigan Yates, Channel Nine News,
Can you tell us if she knew her killer?"

Yes, I can confirm Mysti was familiar
with her Assailant.

"Oh God, there's a killer in Palm Grove."

The voice came from the back of the
ever- growing crowd, came from Arayah

Le Roux motioned for Officer Riley to
come over to him. Riley did so

Le Roux put his hand over the
microphone and said to Riley

"Get her out of here."

By the time Riley got to the back of the
crowd, Arayah was gone

Riley threw her arms in the air "This
woman's bloody Houdini"

Riley used the water police boat and went
to "River Rose," where she found Arayah
fishing off the stern."

"What are you doing here?" Riley inquired

"I needed to relax. This is getting all too much. I can't believe Garrett killed Mysti in such a brutal way. I just can't."

"You realize you are a suspect too, don't you?"

Yes, Detective Le Roux said not to leave town. I haven't. I just came out to the boat to clear my head." Arayah said with a sigh.

Meanwhile, Garrett was getting tired of all the questions and accusations.

Either I am under arrest or let me go," to which Le Roux replied

"I'll let you go when I am good and ready, not before."

There was a knock on the door. It was Holloway. He was speaking to Le Roux in a tone that was a whisper.

"It wasn't him; The DNA doesn't match, It wasn't Arayah," he continued,

"Ready for the kicker? - It was Maverick"

"You've got to be kidding me. You mean to tell me an 80-year-old weakened man brutally murdered a woman 40 years younger than him?" Le Roux said with a slight chuckle

"Where is he now?" asked Holloway inquired "I Don't Know," he replied

"You are free to go, Arayah, but you still have to face the evading police and to pervert the course of justice charges," Le roux said as he stood up to leave.

Twenty minutes later, a full-scale search and APB (All points bulletin) was deployed to find Maverick.

Maverick was not found locally; it appears he has successfully evaded police.

It wasn't until Pol Air located a run-down shack in the Marramarsh national park that this Shack appeared to be his hideout while on the run.

On a cold and wet Thursday morning at around 10 am, a team of ten armed members of the police force, headed by Superintendent Holloway, surrounded the Shack, deep in the Marramarsh National Park.

Holloway ordered the removal of four campers who were staying nearby out of the area as a matter of safety,

Using Army sign language, Holloway instructed Le Roux's men to move in.

Taking things slowly so they didn't startle Maverick

They had to be careful. They all knew Maverick was violent and was well aware of what he could do.

Riley approached the front door and was surprised to find the door ajar and Maverick sitting at the Dining table as if he were expecting someone to enter the door at any minute.

Riley had turned slightly to signal to Le Roux when suddenly everything went black. Slowly she fell to the ground.

Screaming and yelling followed shortly after as Le Roux made his way to Riley, He Called an ambulance on his radio

while Holloway tackled Maverick to the ground.

"Maverick William Jacobson, you are under arrest for the Murder of Mysti Renee Dawkins and the attempted Murder of Officer Riley Sanders. You have the right to remain silent. Anything you can and will be used against you in a court of law. You have the right to an attorney. If you cannot afford an attorney will be appointed for you.

Do you understand these rights I have just read you?

Do you wish to speak to me with these rights in mind?"

Maverick's only two words he spoke were,

"No Comment"

Holloway, Handcuffed Maverick, lifted him off the ground, and escorted him to the car just as the ambulance arrived.

After securing Maverick in the squad car, Holloway walked over to Riley and Le Roux, kneeling beside her, holding pressure on her Left shoulder to stem the flow of blood that was flowing faster than he could imagine.

"How's she doing?" Holloway asked

She's losing a lot of blood, Sir; I can't stop it. It just keeps coming" by now, Le Roux's uniform is covered in the blood of Officer Riley.

Riley opened her eyes long enough to ask what happened, and if we got him, Le Roux was about to reply to her before she fell unconscious again.

Byron and Taylah, the two ambulance officers, assessed Riley's injuries, checking her oxygen levels, heart rate, and blood pressure, and placed a central line in her arm to administer drugs and blood, if necessary,

Byron and Taylah gently placed Riley on a stretcher and put her in an ambulance before racing to the hospital.

Holloway went back to Redmead police station while Le Roux followed the ambulance to Dullich Base Hospital, where Riley was being taken; Le Roux followed them into the Emergency Department before being stopped by a Nurse who told him he had to wait in the waiting room.

She's my partner; I need to be with her." "No, you must wait here; let us do our work."

Le Roux was found pacing up and down the corridor by Holloway,

"Any word on how Riley is yet?"

No Sir, nothing; Travis could feel tears starting to well up and sting his eyes, he had to stay strong, but it's hard when your partner of 15 years is lying in a hospital bed, not knowing if she is dead or alive.

"Make my words, Sir, if Riley dies, Maverick is finished. DO YOU HEAR ME, FINISHED"

"Calm yourself, Travis. This is not the time nor the place for outbursts, Holloway said

Travis started to walk towards Emergency when he noticed a doctor approaching him; he stopped and outstretched his hand; the Doctor, a woman who was 28 years old, of Native American heritage, long black hair tied back in a ponytail, had introduced herself, good morning I'm Dr. Lavinia freeman as she shook Le Roux hand.

Officer Riley is heading up to surgery; she has an Axillary Artery injury to her left shoulder; we managed to retrieve the bullet; she continued as she handed Holloway the jar the shell was contained in, "it looks like a slug from a Glock 23 Gen 4, you'll have to get the fire-arms lab to confirm it though". Lavinia concluded as she walked away.

Back at Redmead, Arayah was waiting for Garrett to come and pick her up.

Garret walked in the front door and went to the reception to ask where his Girlfriend was,

"Honey," Arayah said as she got up to walk over to him.

Garret embraced Arayah and kissed her on the Forehead.

"Are you OK? How was it?" he inquired "It was awful; they bought Maverick in, in

handcuffs, he was bloodied and bruised; oh

Garrett, I think Maverick Killed Mysti," she cried

"Don't cry, Babe, it will be OK, I promise." "You can't know that, can you?" she sobbed As they walked out of the police station

They noticed Holloway and Le Roux walking towards them; there was blood on Le Roux's uniform and asked what had happened.

Neither Holloway nor Le Roux said anything. They just kept walking.

I wonder what happened, Arayah thought

It was getting late; Garrett asked Arayah if she wanted to go out for tea as he was too tired to go home and cook; Arayah shrugged her shoulders, "yeah, I suppose we should eat something" with that, they got in "Shorty" and

drove to the local pub for and ordered a counter meal.

Garrett and Arayah arrived at his place at around 10 pm to find that the front door was open, the lounge room trashed, like someone had been looking for something, but what?

Arayah started cleaning up while Garrett went outside to check the perimeter in case someone was still around; Garrett stopped in his tracks when he noticed the light to the back shed was on strange; I swear I turned the lights off before, he thought. Walking over to the shed to turn the light off and go back inside.

Arayah had finished cleaning the lounge room and headed to the bathroom to shower.

She switched the light on and noticed something written in blood on the mirror;

it was then she screamed; Garrett ran to the bathroom

"WHAT'S WRONG" he yelled

Arayah looked white as a sheet and pointed to the mirror.

"YOU WILL PAY FOR WHAT YOU HAVE

DONE" Blood dripped down the vanity mirror.

"Who could have done this?" Garrett said

"I don't know, but I'm not staying here tonight; take me home," Arayah begged

The fading crime scene tape was still wrapped around the fence at Evergreen Hills when they drove past on their way to Arayah's house.

Arayah and Garrett went inside and lay on the couch with the television on.

The following day Garrett was up and making breakfast when they heard a knock at the door,

Arayah got up to answer it and was shocked to find who was at the other side of the door.

"What are you doing here, she asked I thought you had been arrested."

Garrett peered over his shoulder

"Good to see you again; want some breakfast?" he asked

The other person came inside, "yeah, that'll be nice, thanks, mate," he said as he sat at the kitchen table

"Who is this, Garrett?" Arayah inquired With a slight giggle, he said, "this is Mitchell Maverick's twin brother".

"Wait, What," she said, surprised. "I didn't know Maverick had a twin,

"Obviously, Maverick never mentioned me Mitchell said sadly. He still doesn't want to know me; he just can't let go of the past."

"Will someone please tell me what's going on"

Arayah demanded

"OK, where do I start" Mitchell began
When we were young, maybe 11 or 12,

something terrible happened to Maverick;
we

were racing our quad bikes in
MarraMarsh national park when
Maverick lost control and flipped; the
impact from him hitting the ground
caused him to lose consciousness.

I left him there alone, so I could get help,
but when we returned, he wasn't there,

We searched for days, even weeks, but
we couldn't find him; we appealed to the
public for help finding him, but there was
nothing, no clue as to where he was.

Mum, Dad, and I had given up hope of
finding him; as the years passed, we felt
sure he was dead

Then one day, unexpectedly, he turned up
at mum and dad's house.

We asked him what happened and where
he was for all those years, he said

someone had found him and taken him to the old Shack, but Maverick couldn't tell anyone, what his name

was because the injury to his head gave him amnesia, the person who helped him died and left him the Shack, that's where he had been living.

"Didn't you check the shack while searching for him?" Arayah inquired

"We didn't know it was there; it was hidden by trees and scrub," Mitchell replied

"I had no idea where he went after he left mum and dad's house until I heard on the news that he had been arrested for Murder."

After finishing Breakfast, Garrett, Arayah, and Mitchell decided they would sit on the back porch, enjoy the peaceful surroundings with a beer, and engage in general chatter.

They hadn't been there long when there was a knock on the door. Garrett got up, walked over to the front door, and opened it,

He gasped in horror when he saw who it was,

"It can't be she's dead, I Kill-" he stopped abruptly

"Who is it, babe," Arayah asked as she walked over to Garrett, Arayah too, was in shock,

They were both looking at a woman with curly blonde hair, brown eyes, and an olive complexion. She looked exactly like Mysti,

But Mysti was dead; how is that possible?

Arayah wondered

"Right, boys, we have what we need," the woman said, removing her wig. It was Raquel, the crime scene agent.

"Garrett William Jarvis, you are under arrest for the Murder of Mysti Renee Dawkins and conspiring to commit Murder," Le Roux stated

"You have the right to remain silent. Anything you can and will be used against you in a court of law. You have the right to an attorney. If you cannot afford it, an attorney will be appointed for you."

"Do you understand these rights I have just read you?"

"Do you wish to speak to me with these rights in mind?""

"Yes" was the only reply Garret spoke

Arayah was wailing when she demanded to know why they were arresting Garrett.

"What are you doing? Maverick killed Mysti, not Garrett."

"Maverick told us everything," Raquel told Arayah

"No, it's not, he wouldn't have, he can't have, he wasn't even."

"Stop talking, you stupid bitch," Garrett yelled

But it was too late. Arayah had already said too much, and Raquel had heard it all; in fact, Holloway had heard it too. He listened in on the entire proceedings as Raquel wore a hidden microphone.

Back at Redmead Station, Garrett was photographed, fingerprinted, and formally charged with Murder and conspiracy to commit Murder before being escorted into the interview room by Detective Travis Le Roux

"Here we go again," Garrett said with a sigh

Le Roux turned on the tape recorder and stated

"Please state your name and address for the recording."

"Garrett William Jarvis, 2932 Bottle brush Road Palm Grove NSW," he replied

"Let's take it from the top. Tell me about what happened to Mysti." Le Roux said

"It was Thursday night, Garrett began

"I was lying in bed, trying to sleep. I had a pretty big night previously; I didn't get home til about 2am. Peanut, my foxie, was barking his head off; I let him out, thinking he wanted to go to the toilet, and he ran straight to the Evergreen Hills. As I approached the main gate, I heard a scream; it sounded like it had come from a woman. I wanted to investigate, but Peanut yelped and came running back to me, so we left, came home, and went back to bed.

"Can anyone confirm this?" Le Roux interjected

"Not Likely; I was at home alone with Peanut. I didn't see anyone til around 7pm Friday night when I went to the Driftwood hotel." Then, Garrett continued, I saw Arayah and asked her if she heard a scream from Evergreen Hills.

She said she hadn't, so we went to investigate.

When we got there, we saw flames behind the main building,

We assumed it was pallets and rags burning, as that is what we say in the pile that was still smoldering away.

We looked for something to put the fire out with, and that's when I found Mysti's head in the bucket.

We were going to leave to get help when we noticed a shadow in the doorway; it was Maverick.

"Why didn't you call the police and stay at the scene? Le Roux asked

"Me, damn mobile was flat coz I left the torch on. Garrett reiterated. So, Maverick went to get help in my truck."

"That's it; that's all I can tell you," Garrett concluded

"Interview suspended at 3:45pm; spoke Le Roux into the microphone as He pressed stop on the recorder.

Raquel pressed Arayah for answers when Le Roux walked into the interview room.

"Right, Arayah, here's the skinny; Garrett told us his version, so I want to hear yours' can you do that? Le Roux questioned

"That Thursday night, I was at the Driftwood hotel with a group of people; I was getting pretty drunk and decided it was best to walk him; it wasn't that far; I've walked home many times before.

As I walked home, I noticed Garrett driving past; he had someone else in the truck. I just figured he was dropping a mate off at home. I

was almost home, so I didn't see the point in flagging him down.

"The next night, Friday, I saw Garrett at the tree, and he asked if I had heard a scream; he said it sounded like a woman's scream. I said I hadn't as I was asleep when Garret claimed to hear the scream."

"We then got into his truck and drove to Evergreen Hills; we noticed flames behind the main building when we got there. We looked for something to put the fire out, but I wasn't having much luck. Garrett found something, I assumed, put the fire out with; as I went to walk towards Garrett, he told me to stay where I was and that I didn't want to see what he had found."

"We were about to leave when we noticed the shadow in the doorway; Garrett told me to shut up and keep walking til He realized it was Maverick."

"We were both somewhat relieved; I thought it was maybe the murderer."

"Garrett and Maverick took me back to the truck and told me to wait."

"I did for a while, and curiosity got the better of me because I got out of the truck and headed towards the skip bin; using my mobile

phone torch, I looked inside, and that's when I saw the severed head."

"I knew who it was when I saw her face. The final look on her face was one of sheer terror."

"How did you know, Mysti?" Raquel Asked

"Five years ago, I was in a Bi-Sexual relationship with Mysti: we were dating for two years before we broke up."

"I can't remember why we broke up; I don't think it was for any major reason."

"After I started dating Garrett, Mysti began stalking us, almost daily, "

"I would get messages on our phones or find flowers on our doorstep. When we were together, Mysti would buy me three purple roses on her payday."

"I ran into her one day and asked her to stop stalking Garrett and me. I loved her, but not enough to stay."

"Mysti wouldn't listen; she kept staling us, even after I said I would go to the police,

"I eventually told Garrett, what was happening, After Mysti slashed his tires."

Garrett told me not to worry; he would sort it out; I didn't know what he meant. After that,

He never spoke about it again; until now, I just wanted her to stop; I never wanted her dead.

"Oh, God, He killed her," Arayah cried.

Le Roux and Raquel spoke quietly and briefly and decided to let Arayah go. It seemed she had no knowledge of what Garret was planning or doing.

Le Roux returned to Garrett in the interview room

While pressing record on the tape recorder, Le roux stated, "interview resumed at 5:15pm:

"Right, Garrett, what happened that Thursday night: How 'bout the truth this time?"

"As I said before," Garrett began

"I was drinking at the Driftwood Hotel; it was around Midnight or maybe closer to 1am. I was driving home when I noticed Mysti walking toward Evergreen Hills animal sanctuary.

I stopped and picked her up.

"I decided as soon as she got in my truck, Mysti would never see the light of day again; I was going to murder her."

"We drove to the rear of the main building, got out of the truck, and went into the operating theatre."

"I was pretending to be sexually aroused to make Mysti think we would have sexual intercourse."

"I told her to get undressed and lay on the operating table; she did but sat up again, as the table was too cold to lay on. So, I looked around for something to lay on the table; I found an old rug under the sink and laid it on the table; Mysti then laid down, stark naked, and closed her eyes."

"I stood back, admiring her naked beauty."

"I began caressing her nipple with my right hand while reaching under the table for the scalpel; I then took the scalpel and sliced a deep gash in her lift cheek, just below her eye."

Mysti screamed, "Son of a bitch, Garrett, that hurt."

"I then put my hand over her mouth and nose, blocking her oxygen off; as she was struggling to breathe, I sliced her again, and again, I noticed tears coming from her eyes, but I didn't care; I wanted her to suffer, the way she had made Arayah suffer."

"How did that make you feel? Le Roux inquired"

"Alive and exhilarated, almost free, I am the master.

Le Roux's face turned into a grimace as he listened to Garrett's recounting the events at Evergreen Hills; he was appalled but couldn't show it.

Garrett continued

"It wasn't until Maverick came in that I thought I should just stop and let her go. But He came in to help me."

"You mean to say Maverick aided you in Murdering Mysti?" Le Roux exclaimed.

"Yeah, He did; I'm just as surprised as you are, let me tell ya."

Le Roux suspended the interview recording and left the room in a hurry, Locating Raquel in the evidence room when Le Roux walked in and informed her to obtain a warrant for the arrest of Maverick.

"What's going on, Sir?" Raquel inquired

Maverick is an accomplice in the Murder of Mysti Renee Dawkins.

We need to find him NOW!

Returning to Garrett, Le Roux resumed the interview.

"Garrett, tell me what Mavericks involvement is."

"Maverick came in and held Mysti down while "I cut her up.""

"What happened next?" Le Roux asked

"Can I have something to eat?" Garrett inquired

Just as Le Roux was about to get up, there was a knock at the door.

It was Raquel with the warrant for the arrest of Maverick.

While you are there, can you get Garrett a meal, please?

Le Roux returned to sit and listen to the rest of Garret's statement.

"Mysti was lying on the table, lifeless; she was still breathing, but she wasn't moving anymore.

Maverick handed me the bone saw and said, "Here, use this?"

"I grabbed the saw and started hacking at her legs; blood poured out of her like someone left a tap on. "

"The sight of the blood made me feel like I was drunk; it was an amazing rush."

Le Roux, feeling sick to his stomach at how this Heinous crime was such a joyous event to Garrett, wondered how he could continue this interview.

There was another knock at the door; Garrett's meal was delivered this time.

While Garrett was eating, Le Roux left the room to take a phone call.

It was Dullich Hospital with news of Riley, which wasn't good.

The bullet that had ripped through her Axillary Artery caused an inoperable injury to her left shoulder; unfortunately, Riley will lose the use of her left arm due to the shooting.

Dr. Freeman explained that Riley would recover fully and need to be on light duty for the near future.

Le Roux felt relieved; his partner was going to be OK; now we needed to get her back on deck.

Garrett had finished his meal when Le Roux returned to the interview room.

"Ready to go again, Garret?" Le Roux questioned.

Garrett belched and continued his interview.

"It wasn't until I sliced her throat, oh her pretty little throat, it was so soft and without any marks on it……. well, that was until I dragged the scalpel from one side of her throat to the other; he chuckled.

"Maverick was taking the pieces of Mysti and throwing them in the skip bin; strangely, He seemed as excited as I was."

He was throwing rags and disused pallets into a pile and set them on fire; Maverick said if we burned her body parts, there would be no trace of her, and we would be in the clear.

"After I sliced her throat open, I got the bone saw and started moving it back and forth until the jagged edges of the saw hit the table with a dull ting; it was then I knew I had completely severed her head from her body.

"I wasn't yet satisfied; I wanted to play more; I had to keep going til the job was done.

"What happened next?" Le Roux asked

"Well," continued Garrett, "After I sliced that bitch to bits, I throw the bone saw in the sink, got her body parts and threw them all over the place, her head got thrown in the skip bin, her

torso was thrown out in the back of the yards, and Maverick threw the rest of her in the fire,

"Are you saying Maverick was an accomplice in destroying evidence?" Le Roux inquired in a state of shock.

"Yeah, that's what I am telling you," Garrett responded

"I grabbed a quick shower when I got home and went to the hotel and met up with Arayah and the others," Garrett concluded.

The following day Detective Le Roux Arrested Maverick for being an accomplice to murder.

It would be 2 weeks before Garrett and Maverick appeared in the Dullich Courthouse to answer the charges of Murder.

The courtroom attendance cheered as the jury red the Guilty on all counts to Maverick and Garrett.

Arayah was broken and sobbed through the entire proceedings.

Le Roux stood up and turned around to leave when he noticed a familiar face sitting on the bench near the back of the courtroom; it was Riley; as Le Roux approached her, with a smile on his face, Riley got up and stepped backward and walked out the door.

Le Roux called, "Hey Riley?" but Riley kept walking.

Wondering what that was all about, Le Roux went to his squad car. Under the windscreen wiper, he found a note in a red envelope addressed to him; he took the letter, put it in his pocket, and got in his car.

Le Roux arrived home a short time later to find Riley in his driveway.

He flashed his headlights as he drove into the driveway and parked behind Riley, essentially blocking her in; he was going to get to the bottom of the anonymous letter. He sat in his car and pulled out the letter,

Travis, he read

I am writing to let you know that I am pregnant with your child; I don't want or need anything from you; I will bring this child up on my own, I felt you should know that you are going to be a father.

Regards Arayah

What did I just read, Le Roux pondered, how could this happen, we only met up once after Garrett was arrested, and it was only brief.

Oh God what am I going to do now. Le Roux wondered as He looked up and saw Riley standing in front of his car. He gave her a slight smile and unbuckled his seat belt, opened the door, and got out.

"Riley, Good to see you again, how are you?" he remarked as he went to kiss her on the cheek.

Riley pulled away slightly "Don't you dare,

Travis Just don't" she cried

"Wait, what's going on babe?" Le Roux

demanded.

"How could you, we've been together 15 years, and not once have you ever slept with a suspect. So why did you do it?"

"You were in the hospital on life support, Arayah was distraught by Garrett's arrest and Mysti's death, things lead to things and now… Oh Hell I've made a terrible mess of things, Le Roux said feeling sorry for himself.

Riley and Travis walked inside, sat on the lounge, and talked until the wee hours of the morning.

It was the first time in a long time that they could have a deep and meaningful talk.

Later that morning Riley and Travis went in to work, it was then they learned the fate of Garrett and Maverick.

Garrett was sentenced to life behind bars, with no possibility of parole for the Murder of Mysti.

Maverick was sentenced to 30 years in jail for being an accessory in the murder of Ms Dawkins.

Arayah was given a community service order and was put on home detention for 2 years, with the exception to give birth in a hospital, where she will then return home.

Riley and Travis Got Married 6 months later and retired to the country with their 3 dogs.

Mitchell was able to find full-time work and accommodation, He lived to the age of 95.

The End